Ladybug's Christmas

Written and Illustrated by
Anabella Schofield and Sofia Schofield

pink umbrella
books

PHOENIX, AZ

To our parents—thank you for inspiring, encouraging, and believing in us. We love you!

ISBN: 978-1-949598-16-2

Published by Pink Umbrella Books (www.pinkumbrellapublishing.com)

Anabella Schofield- author

Sofia Schofield- author

Ladybug's Christmas / Anabella Schofield and Sofia Schofield.

When preparations for a Christmas feast go wrong, Ladybug remembers the importance of togetherness during the holiday season.

ISBN : 978-1-949598-16-2

Illustrations by Anabella Schofield and Sofia Schofield

Illustrations © 2020 Anabella Schofield and Sofia Schofield

Cover design © 2020 Adrienne Quintana

In the garden on a cold winter's day,
Ladybug happily worked away.

Wrapping a present with the utmost care,

Ladybug watched snowflakes
drift through the air.

Suddenly, Dragonfly appeared at the window,

Carrying a package tied up with a bow!

To Ladybug's delight,
Dragonfly wasn't gliding by.
She was on her way to deliver a pie!

Opening the door with joy, Ladybug cried,

"Come in, my dear friend,"
and Dragonfly flew inside.

"Thank you for the pie!"
Ladybug said with a smile.
"Would you like to stay
and visit for a while?"

"Of course!" Dragonfly agreed,
so they sat together,

Enjoying slices of pie
and the snowy weather.

All too soon,
Dragonfly had to depart.

Ladybug thanked her friend
with all of her heart.

While washing the dishes in the kitchen sink,
She spied her cookbook and started to think.

"A Christmas feast for my friends to eat!
Oh, how fun! Wouldn't that be sweet?"

Ladybug wrote a list
of all the guests to invite,

Then asked each one,
"Can you come over tomorrow night?"

Ladybug picked up
her cookbook once more,
Selecting recipes she knew
her guests would adore.

Next, she recorded
what she would need
In order to make
her Christmas feast succeed.

Gathering her bags to bring to the store,
She put on her scarf and flew out the door!

Ladybug gazed at the glorious scene,

A white winter's blanket
over the garden, once green.

Flying gracefully to the little shops below,
She admired the sparkling lights aglow.

Ladybug flew down every aisle,
Greeting each bug with a wave and a smile.

Carrying her groceries and leaving the mall,
Ladybug wished a wonderful Christmas to all.

Arriving home as the night grew late,

Ladybug yawned, "Tomorrow, I'll decorate!"

When she arose the next morning,
Ladybug was very excited!

She looked forward to seeing
the guests she'd invited.

"Where shall I begin?" she thought to herself,

Pulling her cookbook down from the shelf.

She whipped up some dishes,
then sat down to rest.

But a knock on the door
filled her with stress!

"Oh, dear!" Ladybug said in dismay.
"No one should be here 'til later today!"

But what could she do? She invited them in.
They started to sing. Honeybee played violin!

Ladybug clapped when
they finished their song,

But rushed to the kitchen
to find something was wrong!

Ladybug blinked back the tears in her eyes.
"This is such a disaster!" she apologized.

"It's okay!" Snail said, and the others agreed.
"We'll help you with whatever you need!"

Ladybug turned on her
favorite Christmas tunes,
Then joined her friends
to blow up balloons.

Butterfly and Ladybug
set the table with care,

While Ant, Caterpillar, and
Dragonfly decorated with flair.

Grammy Bug made sandwiches
that were sure to satisfy,
And Honeybee and Snail
served up slices of leftover pie.

With the feast finally ready,
they gathered by the tree,

Enjoying the food and, most of all,
each other's company.

For Ladybug knew
togetherness at Christmastime
Truly made the holiday season sublime.

The
End

CPSIA information can be obtained
at www.ICGtesting.com
Printed in the USA
LVHW010352281120
672813LV00014B/241